Palo's World
Introduction

Over one hundred years ago, the Palos Verdes Peninsula was one large piece of property, the Rancho Palos Verdes. There were a few dirt roads, no trees, and only wild birds and animals. My grandfather, Frank A. Vanderlip, Sr., was a banker in New York, and always looking for a good investment. He put together a syndicate of investors and bought the ranch in 1913, before he had even seen it. When he came out, he fell in love with the area, and envisioned it as a new Riviera. He built himself a big white clapboard house in Portuguese Bend, known as the Cottage, or the Ranch House, for visits with his family of six children. With my grandmother, Narcissa, and the help of professionals, he designed roads, planted trees, and planned new communities. My grandfather loved birds, and found this was a perfect place to start a bird collection. He built an aviary on a gentle slope with room-sized cages, each with rock formations, perches, pools, and a rivulet with little waterfalls connecting each pool. He also had birds that didn't need to be cooped up, swans that swam in a lovely half-circle pond he created, and chickens, bantams, geese, ducks and Guinea fowl. He even had a talking parrot and a monkey. But what thrilled him most were the peacocks.

After the Depression, the bird collection was given to Frank's friends, the Wrigley Family in Catalina, for their aviary. The pair of white peacocks, a delicate species, did not survive. But the twenty-four peacocks that lived loose around Frank Vanderlip's property had chicks, their chicks had chicks, and their families thrived. I never met my grandfather, who died in 1937, but when I was little, I played with my brother in the abandoned birdcages and around the empty bird pond. And I grew up with wild peacocks, and loved them too. I must have been six years old when my mother made me my favorite Halloween costume, a peacock dress of turquoise chiffon, and a little crown. Because I heard them squawk as a child, I never paid any attention to their sound, which some find scary or irritating. We used to get a kick out of houseguests who would tell us in the morning that they had heard a woman screaming for help in the night, when it was only a peacock.

Now the descendants of my grandfather's peacocks have inspired *Palo's World*. I am so happy that the children who are lucky enough to grow up in Palos Verdes, or come visit here, and children everywhere, can learn about peacocks through this book. There are few creatures in nature with such complex beauty. It is a great privilege be able to spot one perched in a tree, strutting on a lawn, or fanning its stunning tail, and to grow up hearing their calls, knowing their sounds are a part of nature around us.

Narcissa Vanderlip
Palos Verdes, January 2012

PALO'S WORLD

by Mary Jo Hazard

illustrated by Jason Norton

Requests for permission to make copies of any part of the work should be submitted online at info@mascotbooks.com or mailed to Mascot Books, 560 Herndon Parkway Suite #120, Herndon, VA 20170.

PRT0412A

Printed in the United States

ISBN-13: 9781937406714
ISBN-10: 1937406717

www.mascotbooks.com

Palo the peachick slipped under the fence.

Palo stamped his tiny foot and chirped. "Mother, wait for me! Look at me!" His mother turned and smiled.

His two sisters giggled and ran down the canyon path. "Come back," Palo's mother called. The naughty chicks didn't listen.

Seconds later, the chicks screamed, "Mother! Help! Help!" The mother peahen raced after her chicks.

Suddenly the peahen stopped. "My babies!" she cried. Palo trembled with fear.

"Get back," a fierce coyote growled. "Get back!"

The coyote snatched the smallest chick and dashed into the brush.

That night the family snuggled together.
"The neighborhood is full of danger for peacocks,"
the mother peahen sadly told Palo and Nya. "You're
safe now, babies. Go to sleep."

A few weeks later, the chicks followed their mother to their favorite yard.
"Your wings are strong," Palo's mother said.
"Who wants to fly?"

"I do! I do!" Palo said.
He flapped his wings as
hard as he could and ...
"I'm flying!" Palo shouted.
"Look at me! Look at me!"

HONK! HONK! HONK!
SQUAWK! SQUAWK! SQUAWK!
"Quick, Devi," Palo yelled to his friend.
"We'll be safe in the canyon!"

Palo and Devi grew older. "Why don't people like us, Devi?" Palo asked. "Some do," Devi said. "Robbie gives us treats."

One afternoon, Palo and Devi watched Robbie play basketball. The ball rolled off the court next to an angry snake.

"Robbie!" Palo cried. He grabbed the snake and shook until it was still. Then he threw it on the ground.

"That snake can't hurt Robbie now," Palo said. Devi smiled. "You're so brave, Palo."

Palo practiced his peacock cry every day. "AARONDT! AARONDT! LOOK AT ME! LOOK AT ME!"

The peacocks answered Palo with ear-splitting cries. The people covered their ears.

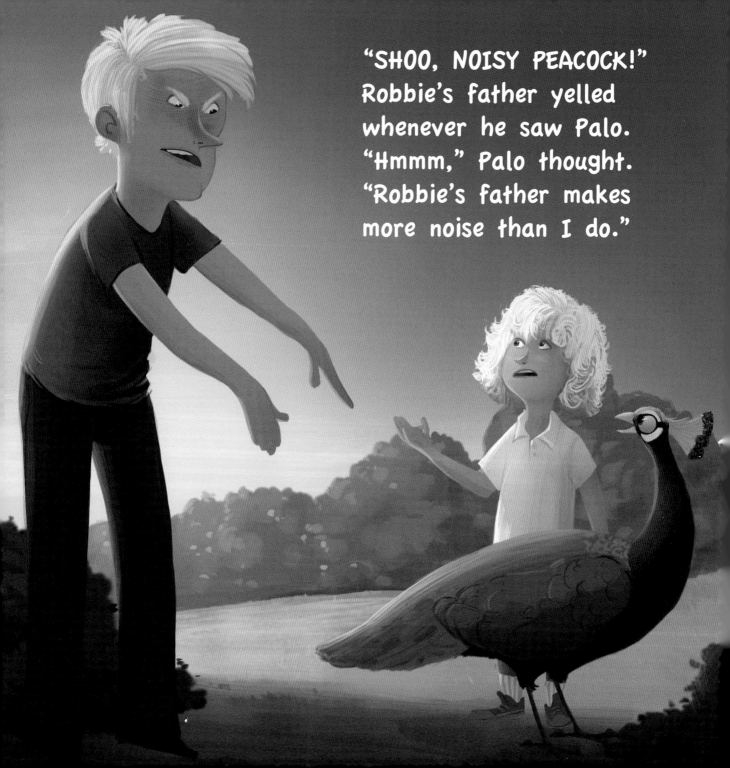

"SHOO, NOISY PEACOCK!" Robbie's father yelled whenever he saw Palo. "Hmmm," Palo thought. "Robbie's father makes more noise than I do."

At night, Palo roosted in Robbie's pine tree.
Palo's friends roosted there too.

The peacocks talked and laughed about peacock things until Robbie's father banged on his bedroom window. "Be quiet. Stop that noise!"

One morning before dawn, Palo blinked. Hot ashes burned his beak. He smelled smoke. It billowed through the pine trees. POP! CRACKLE! POP!

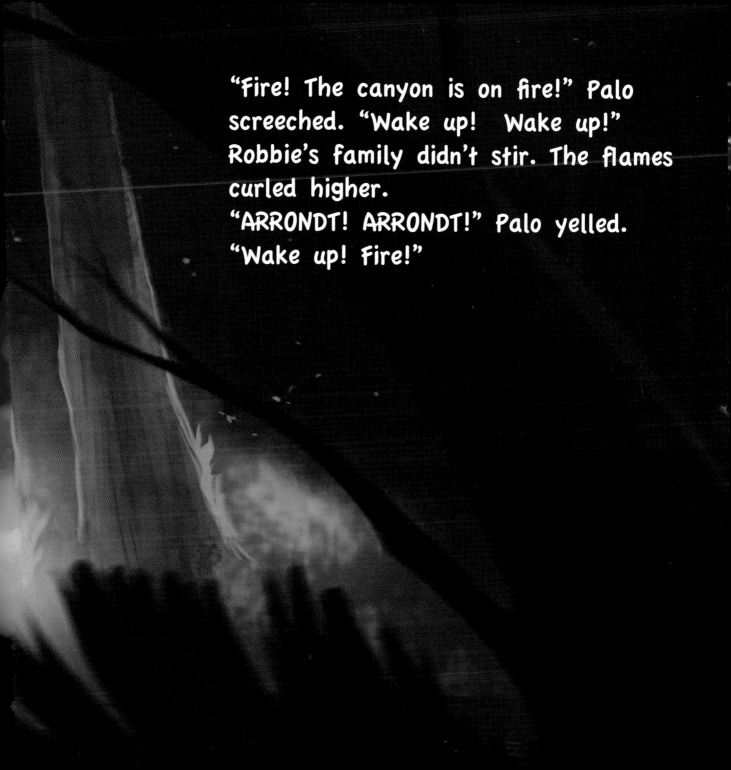

"Fire! The canyon is on fire!" Palo
screeched. "Wake up!   Wake up!"
Robbie's family didn't stir. The flames
curled higher.
"ARRONDT! ARRONDT!" Palo yelled.
"Wake up! Fire!"

The fire burned closer.

"Robbie!" Palo shouted. He flew to the window and rapped with his beak. Rat a tat tat. He pounded. RAT A TAT TAT! RAT A TAT TAT!

Robbie's father leaped out of bed. "Everyone out of the house!" he cried. "I'll call 911!"

Palo hurried to where Devi slept. "Devi!" Palo called. "Over here," Devi said. "Your cries woke me, your mother and Nya too. You saved our lives, Palo."

Fire trucks roared into the neighborhood. Helicopters hovered overhead. The exhausted peafowl watched and waited.

Hours later, the fire was out.
People returned to their houses.

"Palo," Robbie's father said, "I'll never shoo you away again. Good job, big fellow. You're a hero!"

Palo shook his feathers into a big fan. "LOOK AT ME!
LOOK AT ME!" The peacocks looked. The neighbors
looked. And Devi looked!

In the spring, Devi scraped a shallow hole and laid four eggs. The chicks hatched one summer morning.

Three babies followed Devi. One chick stayed in the nest. "Mother, wait for me! Look at me!"

Palo beamed with pride.
"ARRONDT! ARRONDT!
LOOK AT THEM! LOOK AT THEM!"

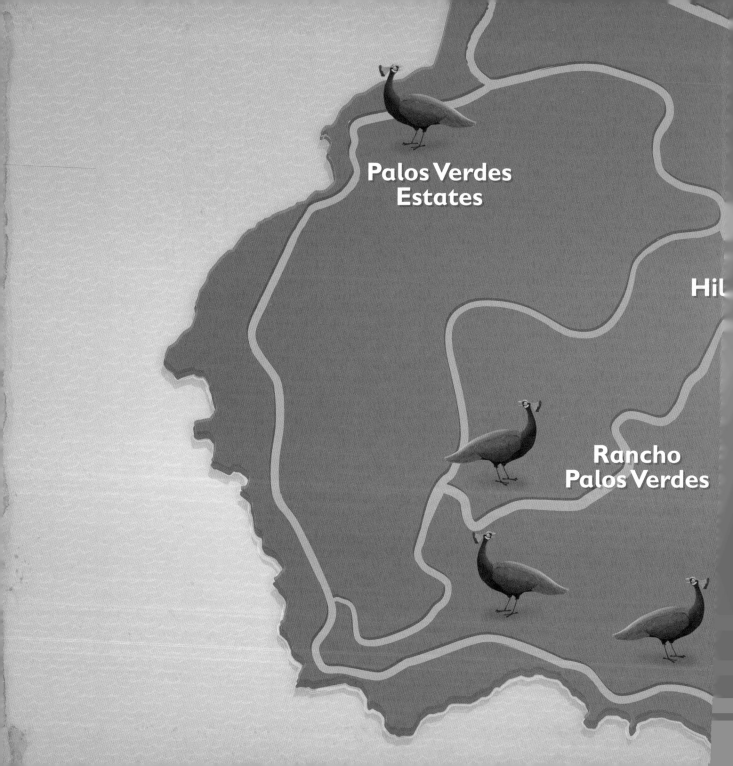

**Palos Verdes
Estates**

Hil

**Rancho
Palos Verdes**